Daddy Ant, You Never Listen!

Written by Sigmund Brouwer

Illustrated by Sharon Dahl

Created by Don Sullivan

Tommy NELSON®

Thomas Nelson, Inc.
Nashville

Lauren

Published in Nashville, Tennessee, by Tommy Nelson®,
a division of Thomas Nelson, Inc.

Scripture quotations used in this book are from the Holy Bible,
New Century Version, copyright © 1987, 1988, 1991 by Word Publishing,
Nashville, Tennessee. Used by permission.

Library of Congress Cataloging-in-Publication Data
Brouwer, Sigmund, 1959-
    Daddy Ant, you never listen / written by Sigmund Brouwer ; illustrated
by Sharon Dahl ; created by Don Sullivan
        p. cm.—(Bug's-eye view books)
    Summary: Daddy Ant, who has had a long day at work, is reluctant to
listen to his family members.
    ISBN 0-8499-7732-0
    [1. Ants—Fiction. 2. Conduct of life—Fiction.] I. Dahl, Sharon, ill.
II. Sullivan, Don, 1953- III. Title. IV. Series.

PZ7.B79984 Dad 2001
[E]—dc21   2001034517

Printed in Italy
01 02 03 04 05 PBI 5 4 3 2 1

The Bible Says . . .

"My dear brothers and sisters,
always be willing to listen . . ."

–James 1:19a

"Daddy Ant," asked Arnie Ant,
"will you listen?"

"Not now," answered Daddy Ant.
"I've had a long day at work.
I want to read the paper."

So Arnie Ant went to Mommy Ant.

"Daddy Ant," asked Annie Ant,
"will you listen?"

"Not now," answered Daddy Ant.
"I've had a long day at work.
I want to read the paper."

So Annie Ant went to Mommy Ant.

"Daddy Ant," asked Baby Ant,
"will you listen?"

"Not now," answered Daddy Ant.
"I've had a long day at work.
I want to read the paper."

So Baby Ant went to Mommy Ant.

"Where is Daddy Ant?" Mommy Ant
asked Arnie Ant, Annie Ant, and
Baby Ant.

"He has had a long day at work,"
they answered. "He wants to
read the paper."

"Daddy Ant," asked Mommy Ant,
"will you listen?"

"Not now," answered Daddy Ant.
"I've had a long day at work.
I want to read the paper."

"Oh," said Daddy Ant. "It's you."

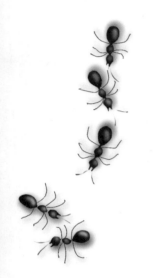

"I've had a long day, too,"
Mommy Ant said.
"Would you please listen?"

Daddy Ant listened.

Daddy Ant listened well.

Let's Talk About . . .

Are you a good listener?

Does anyone at your house forget to listen to others?

Do you listen when someone needs your help?

How can you help others learn to listen to you?

Do all you can to live a peaceful life.
Take care of your own business,
and do your own work as we
have already told you.

−1 Thessalonians 4:11